ROCKY POINT

ROCKY POINT

•

ALICE SHARPE

AVALON BOOKS
THOMAS BOUREGY AND COMPANY, INC.
401 LAFAYETTE STREET
NEW YORK, NEW YORK 10003

PRINTED IN THE UNITED STATES OF AMERICA
ON ACID-FREE PAPER
BY HADDON CRAFTSMEN, SCRANTON, PENNSYLVANIA

This book is dedicated to Joseph Sharpe,
my son and fellow writer

Many thanks and deep appreciation to Arnold Sharpe,
who not only encouraged and advised,
but, as always, provided the inspiration

Chapter One

Catherine Patterson perched on the wide rail surrounding the south deck of the Rocky Point Inn. The deck was unprotected, open to the elements and the sights. Since coming home a year before, she'd fallen into the habit of starting her day this way, reveling in the panoramic view of ocean, beach, and river trapped in early morning mists. If she took deep breaths, she could smell the sea, and sometimes, like today, at this one spot where the railing met the side of the building, an intrepid shaft of summer sunlight challenged the persistent fog. Beside her sat Baloo, the fat white cat who had called the inn home for eight years. His long hair was so clean it was obvious he never stooped to anything as mundane as chasing rodents.

For a second, Catherine's gaze swept by the large improbable shape on the beach, but just as quickly it returned and her eyes widened in amazement. It couldn't be, but already she knew it was. She knew that the foggy swirls hadn't distorted something familiar into something impossible. Even before she set

1

the mug on the railing and turned around, she knew the mists weren't exaggerating a land formation nor were her eyes playing tricks. There was a boat down on the sand where a boat shouldn't be, couldn't be, at least not in one piece.

Baloo jumped for safety as she sprang to her feet, tore open the office door, and, despite the still-slumbering guests, yelled, "Terry, quick. Call Amos and tell him to meet me on the beach. Hurry!"

The door slammed behind her as she raced across the redwood deck and managed the steps. The trail leading down the hill was off to her right; she found it almost unconsciously, following a course she'd helped carve twenty years before when, as a child, she'd roamed the headland.

To a casual observer, her flight may have seemed reckless, but Catherine knew all the crisscrossing paths of Rocky Point Head by heart. And besides, she wasn't the kind to play it safe when someone's life might be in danger. As she took a memorized shortcut, she thought about the treacherous reefs out beyond the breakers. From up at the inn, the boat had looked to be all in one piece, but what would she find when she reached the beach?

Her feet slipped out from under her as she made a tight turn, and she slid a couple of yards through brambles and clumps of wild iris before once again intercepting the path. Scrambling to her feet, ignoring a scratch on her arm and a shoe full of mud, she resumed her flight.

By the time she got to the bottom, her breath was coming in ragged gasps. Clasping her side with her hand, she plowed through the deep sand, her speed increasing when she hit the solid sand of the beach at low tide.

Good thing it was low tide too, she thought as she ran toward the sandy bar at the mouth of the river. At low tide and far down the beach, the river was still twenty feet wide, but its depth shrank to three feet in a narrow channel. For years, Amos had been cursing the ever-increasing shallowness of the river, blaming everything from government bureaucracy to silt to the drought. Because of the low tide, Catherine was able to pull her sweatpants far above her knees, choose which rocks from which to leap, and wade across. She was wet from the waist down, but it didn't matter. Nothing mattered but getting to the boat and making sure no one was hurt.

Once gaining the other side, she allowed herself to slow down. At last, bent over, chest heaving, hands propped on bare knees, she peered through the damp tendrils of her hair at the sight that had brought her crashing down the hill with such urgency.

On the smooth sandy beach before her was a large sailboat. The whole thing, from keel to masts, was sitting at an angle, the bottom of the straight keel somewhat buried in sand, the bow pointing gallantly toward the rocky cliff, a shelf of which almost overhung the end of the long bowsprit. Across the stern, written in jaunty gold leaf, were the boat's name and home port: *Ashanti, Seattle, Washington.*

Catherine's sense of urgency fled as she noted the perfect condition of the boat. The safety equipment— a small upside-down skiff lashed securely to the foredeck and a horseshoe buoy on the stern pulpit— was still in place. Raise the sails, she thought, and the image of a small ship plowing through heavy seas would be complete. Incredible. Not that sailboats were unheard of in Rocky Point Cove—in fact, during the summer months it wasn't unusual to see three or four at a time anchored in the protected waters. It was just that one had never actually washed ashore before like the molted shell of a Dungeness crab.

Just when she was wondering if anyone was still aboard, the hatch opened and out popped a half-naked man clutching his jaw. She watched in silence as the man's gaze traveled from the rocky shelf at the bow of the boat to the stretch of empty beach that separated the stern from the ocean. His expression went from confused to incredulous to horrified. Catherine decided she should announce her presence.

"Hello," she called, approaching slowly. From the ground, the boat looked huge—a small world beached, an ocean-going satellite taken out of orbit, decommissioned. Catherine's head came no higher than the waterline.

The man looked down at her from the deck. He needed a shave, but that did nothing to alter the fact that he was extremely easy to look at. The dark stubble might even add to his general appearance of rugged masculinity, Catherine thought. At any rate, it did nothing to distract from it. He was muscular and tall, the look of health and good genes honed with exercise.

"Hi," he muttered, his voice hoarse.

As she waited, he climbed between the lifelines and lowered himself over the toe rail. He hung by his fingertips for a moment before dropping the rest of the way to the beach, about four feet, in an impressive display of the strength in his shoulders and arms. He landed firmly enough, but again he clutched his face and wailed in pain.

"You're hurt," she said. "Here, sit down. Were you thrown from your bunk or—"

"No, no," he insisted. He tried smiling, but that only made him wince. With a stiff nod at Catherine, he began walking around his boat. Catherine followed.

"It looks as though nothing is wrong with her," she said, admiring his back. He had a splendid back, she decided: tanned, smooth, and muscular without being beefy. Not that his back mattered one way or another.

He turned around and looked at her. "Nothing wrong with her? Excuse me, Miss Boat Expert, but I usually keep her in the water. Sounds strange, I know, but there you are."

Catherine bristled. "No kidding? You mean you don't carry her from beach to beach?"

After a second's hesitation, the hint of a smile played across his lips and he mumbled, "I used to, but the darn thing got too heavy."

Catherine grinned. "What I meant," she began anew, "is that you seem to be extremely lucky. This is the sandiest beach around, which always amazes people because the name of the place is Rocky Point, but all the rocks are out in the reef and under the water—"

She stopped because they'd reached the far side of the boat and he was pointing. What had kept *Ashanti* from tipping over on her side was the one rock on the beach. Unfortunately, the boat had managed to find the worst possible place to perch herself, on a jagged black rock where the most damage could be done.

"What foul luck," she said.

The man sighed deeply, grimaced, touched his face, and muttered something unintelligible.

Catherine said, "Aren't you cold?"

"Huh?"

"Cold?" she prompted. She was shivering, but of course, half her clothes were soaked clear through. Still, she had on a dry sweatshirt and a windbreaker, and he wore only a pair of cutoff jeans.

"No," he said. They walked around to the stern. He turned the propeller absently.

"My name is Catherine Patterson," she told him.

He didn't say anything, so she continued. "I own the Rocky Point Inn. You can see it from here." His gaze followed hers to the top of the headland. The whole inn was visible from this beach: the large main building that housed the dining room, lounge, and offices; the cabins sporting their new coats of bright white paint and pine green trim; the pinks, oranges, yellows, blues, and purples of the garden flowers. For a second, Catherine stared at it. It was her world now, part and parcel, a thought that still startled her.

"It looks nice," the man said.

"Yes. Well, anyway, I was outside this morning when I saw your . . . predicament. I came crashing down here because I was certain someone must have been hurt." She looked at his jaw and added, "Are you sure you're okay?"

"Jake Stokes," he said. "The only thing wrong with me is a little toothache."

"Did something fall on you?"

"No. It's nothing, really."

"Do you realize your jaw is swollen?" She didn't ask him about his dilated pupils or point out that his speech was so slurred he was hard to understand.

"I'm fine," he muttered impatiently. He poked at something in the sand with his toe, then sat down on his heels and dug with his fingers until he uncovered a shiny metallic object. Standing, he pulled on the object and Catherine saw the sand erupt in a long line as a chain sprang from the beach. They both followed the chain to the water's edge; because of the calm sea, there was no surf. Jake pulled until a pile of wet chain lay at his feet and the end dangled from his hands.

A mild oath escaped his lips, then his anger seemed to dissipate. When he spoke, his voice sounded resigned. "Broken shackle," he said. "It was a brand-new Danforth anchor too."

Over Jake's shoulder, Catherine spied Amos approaching, his bowlegged gait as distinctive as a fingerprint.

"Help is on the way," she said.

Their eyes locked for the first time and Catherine felt her breath catch. His were excruciatingly green with sparkling highlights, like the sun streaming through the seawater, catching on waving tendrils of kelp. He had straight black brows and a thatch of short black hair that appeared to have a mind of its own. His jaw was strong and angular on the left side and a little puffy on the right, bristling with two or three days' growth of beard. She was willing to wager a bundle his toothache was a doozy.

"Looks as though I need help, doesn't it?" he said as though the idea was foreign enough to make him feel uncomfortable.

She shrugged, and looked away from his amazing gaze before she lost herself in uncharted waters. If there was one thing she absolutely, positively didn't need at this difficult point in her life, it was a vagabond sailor who couldn't even keep his boat in the water.

Amos was huffing and puffing by the time he reached them. At sixty-six he was overly fond of fried food and slumping in his deck chair while the fishermen who used his dock challenged the high seas and the fish. He ate one meal a day at the inn, and Catherine tried her best to make sure it was low in fat and high in fiber, but he continually thwarted her attempts to reshape his dietary habits.

Amos pushed his filthy captain's hat back on his balding head, hooked his thumbs under the strained waistband of his black cotton work pants, and said, "In all my years on this good earth I thought I'd seen it all, but by golly, this here takes the cake, it really does."

Jake narrowed his eyes.

"Takes a landlubber or one of you sailing buffs to beach a boat like this," Amos continued unmercifully. He chuckled and pointed at the rock. "Found the one place to punch a hole in her too. If you don't get her refloated soon, then you might as well kiss her good-bye, 'cause there ain't much of a beach here come high tide."

Amos imparted this news with his customary lack of tact, made all the worse by the twinkle of glee that danced in his gray eyes. Catherine had learned to take his not-so-gentle ribbing without too much offense, seeing as she'd known him her whole life. But Jake looked as though he'd like to strangle the old man.

"I'm sure he's aware of all this," she said.

"You need help," Amos said.

"No, thanks," Jake mumbled.

"Come on, boy, don't let pride—"

"I said, no thanks." The way he said it—the cadence, the tone, the firmness—caught Catherine's attention and she glanced back at Jake's face. He looked stern and serious, a man not to be toyed with or taken lightly. As she gazed at him, the expression softened and disappeared and he was once again a shiftless boat bum with a whale of a problem.

"So you did," Amos said with a sigh. "Well, it's a public beach, so you won't mind if I go get my deck chair and a couple of cold beers and watch how you go about this, will you?" He chuckled and added, "Hate to miss a good show." Catherine cast Amos a withering glance that bounced off his weathered face with no effect.

"Be my guest," Jake said.

The two men glared at each other for a moment. Just when Catherine was ready to punch them both in their obstinate noses, she heard a baby crying.

"Is there a child aboard?" she asked.

Jake glanced at her. The cry came again, and he shook his head, which seemed to aggravate his toothache. "It's Py," he said, his hand making the familiar trip to his jaw.

He walked toward the bow of the boat. Catherine's gaze followed him until she saw the small Siamese cat sitting on the foredeck. It nonchalantly howled again, then walked along the bowsprit, leaped to the rocky shelf of land, and daintily descended to the beach in three quick movements. The cat rubbed her sleek body against Jake's leg in a proprietary gesture.

"That boy needs help," Amos said quietly.

"Yes, he does, but you've managed to go and make it impossible for him to ask for it," Catherine said. She leaned down and called, "Kitty, kitty." The cat looked at her, but continued wrapping her sinewy body around Jake's legs.

"Wait till he gets this yacht afloat and she starts taking water through that hole in her side," Amos said without moving his lips. "He'll ask."

Catherine stood up. Jake was in the process of hauling himself up to the deck with the same ease with which his cat had descended. As he was purposely ignoring her, Catherine decided she might as well go back up to the inn and help Terry set up the breakfast buffet. As she turned to leave, she heard Amos hollering.

"I've got a small yard in my marina. At high tide, a boat with a deep keel like this can get through."

She didn't wait to see if Jake took Amos up on his offer. She had the feeling the younger man would rather his boat sink to the bottom of the ocean than ask Amos for anything. And the truth of the matter was, she didn't blame him.

Not that Amos didn't mean well, she reflected as she waded back across the river. This time she walked inland to take the gentler trail up the headland, the one that originated near the fish camp. Amos had rented the camp and the adjacent marina—consisting of one floating dock, one pockmarked ramp, and one shed—for years, first from Catherine's father, now from her. Since almost everyone was out fishing this time of day, the camp appeared deserted, just a dusty cluster of trailers, battered recreational vehicles, dilapidated tents, and empty boat trailers. The place was a mess, always had been, and with Amos running it, always would be. That was okay though, she thought as she threaded her way through an empty campsite. The fishermen who frequented this place liked it this way.

The inn, however, was another matter. It too had fallen into disrepair, mostly because Catherine's father hadn't done much to it over the years, preferring fishing to building. Catherine's grandfather had been the developer in the family, a trait that seemed to have skipped generations; now that she had the inn, she was full of plans for renovation, expansion, and renewal.

Until six months before, the reclusive inn had been little more than forty cabins in sound if not inspired condition. Like the camp and the boat yard, Rocky Point Inn had stood for eighty years, handed down from father to son and now to daughter. And in all that time, it had managed to survive with minimal care.

However, times were changing. Along the northern California scenic coast, an inn catering only to diehard fishermen who were willing to make the winding, sometimes bone-chilling drive along miles and miles of lost coastline just to reach a primitive fishing camp or a run-down hotel couldn't make a go of it. Upon inheriting the place a year before, Catherine had started trying to save it the only way she knew how. She'd mortgaged everything and begun the arduous chore of transforming the inn into a pleasant, beautiful spot where city-dwelling tourists—if she could figure out a way to reach them—could relax.

For all the flak she got from the old-timers, you

would have thought she'd started hammering the inn with a wrecking ball, she thought as she leaned over to pick an aluminum can off the abandoned railroad track. As she resumed climbing she admitted a certain annoyance with Amos, who made her feel as though she was desecrating a holy landmark, all because she'd painted most of the cabins and outfitted them with things like flowered curtains and fluffy quilts. She knew he was worried that her scheme would fail; foreclosure meant losing the marina as well as the inn, so she could hardly blame him.

''Is that a boat down on the beach?''

Catherine looked up to the deck where the slender figure of Terry Lyle leaned against the railing. Terry, Catherine's second cousin, was the thirty-three-year-old widowed mother of a nine-year-old boy named Mike. She'd come to work at the inn the first summer Catherine went off to college, and as far as Catherine could tell, her main job was being her father's gofer. One of the first things Catherine had discovered when she came home to manage the inn was that Terry was a whiz with pastries. A promotion now had Terry taking care of the morning repast.

''What's the story?'' Terry asked, her sky-blue eyes wide with curiosity. She had fine bones and small features that missed beauty by a breath but attained pretty with no effort. Today she wore her pale blond hair up on top of her head, and as usual, was dressed conservatively in tailored tan pants, a cream-colored sweater with pink roses embroidered around the neckline, and modest pearl stud earrings.

Catherine climbed the stairs, carefully sidestepping the sunbathing Baloo. "I have no idea. The captain is a surly man with a toothache who doesn't want anyone's help. How's the buffet setting up?"

"Nicely. Cabin 3-A is waiting for their muffins."

"Let's not keep them waiting."

Terry glanced at her watch. "They should be cool by now."

She grinned and added, "Where do you think you're going?"

"To help, of course," Catherine said.

"I know you think this place can't function without you," Terry said, "but don't you think you'd better change clothes and comb your hair before you greet our guests sopping wet and with an old soda can in your hands? What's that in your hair?"

For the first time, Catherine thought about how she must look. She found an iris tangled in her hair and pulled it free. No wonder Jake Stokes had ignored her.

"Oh, and I forgot to tell you that while you were running down the headland, Dr. Prouse came by."

"Derek was here? What did he want?"

Terry laughed. "Oh, I don't know. Maybe he just wanted to catch a glimpse of the woman he loves. I told him you'd be back in a few minutes, but he was off to the hospital. He said he'd come by tonight around seven for dinner."

Catherine shook her finger at Terry. "Don't go around saying Derek loves me," she said.

"Why?"

"Because he doesn't. We're just friends."

"Oh, brother," Terry said, sighing.

"Terry—"

"Okay, okay. But for both our sakes, I hope you understand that bank loan better than you understand men."

"May we drop this subject?" Catherine asked.

"Consider it dropped. By the way, did you hire a new gardener yesterday while I was taking Mike to baseball practice?"

"Yep. He'll start work tomorrow."

"Great. The lupines are threatening to engulf the lower cabins."

Catherine nodded, but her attention had once more drifted down to the sailboat. It was so out of place on the beach. She wouldn't have admitted it, even to herself, but she was also straining her eyes for a glimpse of the boat's captain.

Jake Stokes dropped his two spare anchors over the stern, where they hit the beach below with a resounding thud. He dumped a coil of line over the stern pulpit and then gently lowered the oars. He wished the old man on the beach would go away.

He unleashed the dinghy from the foredeck, not sure how he was single-handedly going to get it to the ground without smashing it. His tooth ached more than it had the day before and every jolt and jar sent spasms of excruciating pain through his face. If it didn't go away soon, he was going to have to give up and go see a dentist. The thought of a dentist fooling around in his mouth made a fine layer of cold sweat break out across his forehead, which Jake quickly attributed to strenuous labor. He vowed again to wait and see what happened—maybe he had a cold or something that had settled in his tooth. He wasn't at all sure colds actually settled in teeth, but it was better than contemplating a dentist.

By tying lines to the bow and stern of the little fiberglass boat and using the main boom, Jake was able to lower the skiff to the beach. He glanced nervously toward the ocean. The tide was on its way in. Within a few hours, it would be licking the keel, and soon after that, if he wasn't successful in getting her re-floated, the now-gentle surf would pound *Ashanti*'s bow into the cliff.

How in the world had he managed to sleep through the grounding of his boat? Two pain pills and the last two inches of whiskey were the obvious answer, but it offended his pride to think he'd been so out of it that he'd let this happen. If he'd run the rest of his life like this, he wouldn't be where he was today, a thought that brought a reluctant smile to his lips as he thought about exactly where he was: grounded on a thirty-eight-foot ketch in a little cove with a belligerent old tyrant standing by to chortle when he messed up.

And then he thought of the woman who had run

down the head in a flurry of compassion. He'd been rude to her, but he'd been in shock at first, and then he'd been in pain. That drop to the beach had cost him more than a little; he admitted to himself that he'd done it to impress her. He should have crawled down slowly like the feeble old man he currently resembled and at least been civil to her. After all, she'd run down the headland and braved icy water to save him, and although it hadn't been necessary, he hadn't even thanked her.

And she was pretty. Okay, he admitted as he threw a life preserver over the side, she was beautiful. He loved it when women's hair was all weather-tangled like hers—she even sported a deep-purple flower imbedded in the glistening black strands—and though she wore baggy sweats, he could tell her figure was trim here and full there, just as he liked it. And her legs! All that had been showing were her calves, but they were splendidly formed. She even had pretty knees and ankles! Her eyes were big and dark and luminous, full of sparkling good humor. She was beautiful, all right, and she probably thought he was a number-one jerk.

Py bounced back on the boat, settled on top of the cabin, and looked at him, her gaze slightly crossed. A long piece of seaweed dangled from her seal-brown mouth.

"It's okay," he mumbled. "You know you're the only girl for me." He rubbed her between her ears and she dropped the seaweed so she could thank him. Come to think of it, her meow did kind of sound like a baby crying. "You just have to understand that once in a while I've got to lust after a beautiful human woman," he said softly. "You know as well as I do that I'm not interested in anything permanent, so settle down." Py made for the hatch and disappeared below decks.

Jake climbed off the boat slowly. The old man was sitting on the rock, peering at the cracked planks.

"I got some old Port Orford cedar in the shed," the man said. "It's been there since Catherine's granddad used to build boats. I bet it would make a great new plank for this tub of yours."

Jake nodded slowly, which reminded him—as if he needed reminding—that his tooth hurt. "Thanks," he said.

He dragged the dinghy down to the surf, then carried down the anchors, the oars, the lines, and the preserver, all of which he loaded aboard. He launched the boat, which made his mouth feel like a punching bag for a heavyweight prizefighter. Then he began the chore of setting the two anchors as far out in the cove as he could, so that as soon as the water raised *Ashanti* from the sand, he could get her off the beach.

It took over an hour, and by the time the last hook was firmly in place, he wished he'd cracked open another bottle of Jack Daniels, purely for medicinal purposes. He didn't normally drink, especially at a time like this, but he didn't trust the pain pills, and aspirin hadn't touched the agony throbbing through his face.

He'd live, he decided. Better to keep his wits about him and get out of this mess.

Catherine watched the crazy sailor row around the cove. If she leaned over the rail, she could make out Amos sitting in his deck chair down on the beach, and she assumed the shiny reflection off something in his hand came from a beer can. She hoped he was keeping his mouth shut, because the more she watched Jake, the more convinced she became that he was operating on automatic, fighting to save his boat before he keeled over from the poison that his infected tooth was undoubtedly spreading throughout his body.

Her reasons for suspecting this were twofold. One, Jake was obviously in excellent physical condition. His shoulders were broad, his waist was trim, his legs powerful, his muscles well developed, and yet he moved slowly, laboriously, carefully. Two, it certainly appeared he knew his way around boats and was committed to *Ashanti*, and yet he'd apparently slept through her beaching, which must really be rankling him now. Catherine was positive his "little toothache" was really an abscessed tooth. She wondered why he wouldn't admit it.

"Men," she said as she shook her head, unconscious of the smile that stole into her eyes as she watched Jake drop the second anchor in the deep dark waters of the cove.

Chapter Two

"What's he doing out there?" Terry asked.

Catherine was back on the deck. She'd torn herself away long enough to help with the buffet. She was able to greet her few guests by name, thanks to a game of association. The couple in cabin 4-B, for instance, had ruddy complexions thanks to either the wind or a fondness for brandy. "Roses in their cheeks" was the expression Terry often used, and since their last name happened to be Moses, which rhymed with roses, ta-dum, she could recall their name. Sometimes it back-fired; most of the time it worked.

The buffet of fresh fruit, hot coffee, and assorted baked goods was served every morning at ten o'clock. By then the fishermen who tended to stay in the as-of-yet unrenovated cabins or the few hardy souls who climbed the trail from the camp down below were long gone after a hurried meal of bacon and eggs—what else? Catherine was free to set out a tasty, beautiful repast for the tourists without getting into an argument with the morning cook, Lester Boggs. Lester had worked from five AM to eight AM for twenty years and Catherine was convinced he distrusted anyone who didn't load up on cholesterol first thing in the morning. She knew he distrusted her and that she'd made it worse by first turning Terry loose and then bringing in André, the new evening chef. Catherine had hired André with the idea of creating a restaurant that would appeal to the community as well as the inn's potential guests, and would bring in additional revenue.

The trick would be making the first payment, due in less than four months, and then the rest of the payments as they came due. A spasm of worry flickered through Catherine's mind, but she resolutely pushed it aside. Worry accomplished nothing; only action would ease the problems facing the inn. And action dictated she be inventive—soon, too—and come up with a way to fill her fancy new rooms.

And how about her personal problems? How long could she avoid Derek Prouse, for instance, and still have him for a friend? She suspected Terry was right, that Derek was interested in more than friendship. How long would he wait for her to make up her mind?

Terry said, ''Are you ever going to answer me?''

''What?''

''That man down there. What in the world is he up to?''

''Oh. I think he's setting those anchors so that when the tide rises he can pull his boat off the beach. That's what it looks like to me.''

It was one o'clock. High tide was at three, which

meant that anytime now things would start to happen. Fingers of foamy surf were already caressing the end of the keel.

There were a million things to do, yet Catherine was unable to tear herself away from the railing. She knew one of the maids hadn't shown up for work, so she should go help make up the rooms. She didn't move. In fact, it wasn't until André's raised, angry voice, complete with a thick French accent, wafted through the front door that she made any effort to move from her vantage point.

"I'll be right back," Catherine told Terry. She hurried into the big kitchen at the back of the dining room. André stood in the middle of the brightly painted room, white hat erect on his noble head, hands propped on waist, drooping black mustache at odds with the flash of fire in his eyes. The object of his scorn cowered against the long stainless-steel counter.

"This . . . this . . . imbecile! I told him to pound the abalone, and what does he do? He beats on it, he punishes it, he . . . he mugs it! One must pound gently, but firmly, with tender taps. How am I to conquer such ignorance?"

"Miss Patterson, I lived here my whole life," Sam said. He was nineteen, with bristly dark hair, an eighteen-inch neck, and biceps the size of Virginia hams, but though the kid easily outweighed the chef by eighty pounds, there was no question who was the boss in the kitchen. "Dad's been getting abalone for years and I've watched him pound it—"

"Heathen!" André interrupted. "Infidel!"

"Listen," Sam said. "You told me to pound it, so I pounded it."

"Like a barbarian! Like a savage!"

"Now, wait a second—"

"Gentlemen," Catherine interrupted. She turned to Sam and said, "Just don't . . . hit it so hard." Before André could continue, she added, "And André, couldn't you just teach him—"

"I am a master chef, not a teacher of brutes—"

"I must insist you not refer to Sam in those terms," Catherine interrupted. She spread her hands imploringly and added, "Listen, André, I told you I'd hire you more experienced help as soon as the restaurant is a going concern. Meanwhile, surely you can cope with a newcomer."

"First I am lured to this . . . this outpost of humanity, and now, to deal with . . . with this demoniacal—"

"André!"

As Catherine watched anxiously, the knot in André's jaw gradually loosened. "Like this," he growled, grabbing the meat pounder from Sam's hand and expertly whacking it down on a slice of abalone. Catherine walked back through the dining room and found herself praying that her temperamental chef would restrict himself to beating on the abalone and not Sam. Terry was waiting by the door to the cocktail lounge.

"Amos wants you."

"He's here?"

"Right outside. He walked up the hill."

"He never walks up the hill. He drives."

"Well, this time he walked," Terry said.

They held this conversation as they moved through the bar and out onto the deck. Amos was standing beside the railing casting occasional surly glances at the pampered-looking couple sitting in wicker chairs they'd pulled against the side of the building, probably because it was warmer out of the wind. Catherine spared her guests her best innkeeper smile, a smile she was beginning to detest, and searched her memory for their names. She came up blank. Something to do with a circus. Her steps faltered for a second as she tried to come up with the proper association. Trapeze? Clowns?

Amos cleared his throat. "Catherine, if you've got a minute?" Catherine met his gaze; what she saw in his eyes propelled her towards him.

"What's wrong?" she asked as she joined him by the railing.

"It's that fool boy," Amos said, sputtering with anger.

"What fool boy?"

"The one in the boat."

"Jake Stokes?"

"Something is wrong with him," Amos mumbled. "He's doing all the right things, but he looks like the devil and he keeps stumbling. I'll tell it to you straight, girl, I'm worried about what's going to happen to him when and if he gets that boat off the beach. And if he doesn't get it refloated, I'm afraid he's going to stay on her too long and end up getting himself killed.''

"He seems a very competent man," Catherine said as she peered over the rail, straining for a look at the boat on the beach. What she saw made her breath catch. The waves were now breaking near the keel and washing up under the boat. There wasn't enough water yet to refloat it, just enough action to grind the wooden hull against the jagged edges of the rock. Two taut lines led from the aft of the boat to the anchors set in the bay. Whether it was because of Amos' uncharacteristic nervousness or the sight of the small boat in the throes of breaking waves, Catherine felt talons of fear scratch their way up her spine.

"What can we do?" she asked.

"He won't take my help. I don't know if he's stubborn or nuts or just plain sick, but he wouldn't let me aboard to help him and now it's too late.''

Catherine looked at the beach again. She knew what Amos meant. The river was too high to wade across; the beach was treacherous.

"It's just too late," Amos said again, almost to himself.

"Not if you crossed the river up by the marina and went down the side of the hill above his boat. You'd end up above the bow," Catherine said.

"There's no decent path up there," Amos reminded her.

"I roamed all over that hill as a kid," Catherine

said. "I can find a way down to that ledge above his boat. Come on. You can get me across the river—"

"Now, hold on," Amos said. "It's getting dangerous down there."

"Listen, Amos. You're the one who came up here all worried. Well, this is the only way we can help this guy. There isn't time to drive to the bridge. Are you going to get me across the river or not?"

He stared at her a moment, then nodded. "Let's go."

Jake locked his irritated sea mate in the cabin where she proceeded to howl in full Siamese voice. By now he was in a haze of pain which was punctuated by excruciating moments of awareness. The seawater was halfway up the keel and the boat was beginning to rock, which put stress against the hull and the cracks in her planking. He was using the electric bilge pump to handle the incoming water, but already it was having trouble keeping up. What would happen when the boat was actually floating and more water found its way inside? Could the electric pump keep up with it? If not, could he handle the manual pump and still get *Ashanti* into the old man's marina? And once there, was it really outfitted to get her out of the water quickly?

He swore under his breath as a wave of nausea washed through him. Why hadn't he used the first hour of this rotten morning to walk back to the marina and check it out? Time had sped by as he set the hooks, but couldn't he have found a few moments to do such a sensible thing? Jake frowned. He wasn't used to second-guessing himself; he wasn't used to indecision. What was wrong with him? Was some of the pain medication still coursing through his veins, muddling his thinking?

The old man had offered to come aboard, but how did you put a seventy-year-old guy who was obviously out of shape on a perilous boat and ask him to manually pump a ton of seawater out of the bilges? Maybe the old man's heart would give out and that would make this fiasco a nightmare. Had he handled it with tact, or as he suspected, had he grumbled and growled?

It was the pain, he thought woodenly as the boat shuddered beneath him. His whole face was sore; his jaw felt as big as a balloon. His hand made a short trip to his face but came away without touching. He was on the brink of admitting there was no such thing as a cold settling in a tooth.

A shower of dirt and small pebbles skittering across the bow startled him. He looked up toward the slope and saw the woman from the morning, the one with the wild hair, only now it was tamed in a neat ponytail. She was wearing white pants smudged with dirt and a red sweater. She called out to him. Jake stood, aware for the first time that sometime during the last few moments, he'd sunk down on the portside cockpit seat.

The woman on the hill moved down the shelf above the bow, another avalanche of pebbles preceding her. He walked toward her, aware the decks were finally beginning to move a little. He had to get back and tighten those anchor lines.

"What are you doing here?" he called, his voice petering out toward the end as pain racked his head.

"Isn't that kind of obvious?" she asked.

"Please be careful," he said as he reached the bow, pointing down. The waves were breaking against the cliff now and white water was boiling under the bow. "If you fall—"

"So you'd better make sure I don't. Listen, we don't have time to argue, do we? Just help me get aboard and I'll show you the way into the river."

He stared at her. She was, if anything, twice as beautiful as he'd remembered her. The memory of her legs, now encased in white cotton, was still vivid. He felt the boat jerk again, and snapped out of his daze. He walked out onto the bowsprit, alarmed at how much *Ashanti* reacted to the shift of his weight. It meant she was dangerously close to being afloat.

"Hurry," she called.

He reached over the stainless pulpit. She was on an overhanging ledge about three feet above him. "Sit down," he said, and was somewhat surprised that she did as he asked without argument.

"Can you slide toward me?" he asked as his hands locked on her ankles.

"Just catch me," she called.

She paused for a second, and he could see a tinge of fear creep over her face. He squeezed her ankles.